Luna and the Big Blur

A STORY FOR CHILDREN WHO WEAR GLASSES

To my wonderful family...
thanks for seeing the beauty in everyday life! — SD

Published by
MAGINATION PRESS
An Educational Publishing Foundation Book
American Psychological Association
750 First Street, NE
Washington, DC 20002

For more information about our books, including a complete catalog, please write to us,
call 1-800-374-2721, or visit our website at www.maginationpress.com.

Editor: Becky Shaw
Art Director: Susan K. White
Printed by Worzalla, Stevens Point, Wisconsin

Library of Congress Cataloging-in-Publication Data

Day, Shirley, 1962-
Luna and the big blur : a story for children who wear glasses / by Shirley Day ;
illustrated by Don Morris.
p. cm.
Summary: A young girl who hates her glasses learns to appreciate them
after spending a day without them. Includes note to parents.
ISBN-13: 978-1-4338-0398-7 (hardcover : alk. paper)
ISBN-10: 1-4338-0398-4 (hardcover : alk. paper)
ISBN-13: 978-1-4338-0399-4 (pbk. : alk. paper)
ISBN-10: 1-4338-0399-2 (pbk. : alk. paper) [1. Eyeglasses—Fiction.]
I. Morris, Don, ill. II. Title.
PZ7.D3325Lu 2008
[E]—dc22   2008017577

10 9 8 7 6 5 4 3 2 1

Luna and the Big Blur

A STORY FOR CHILDREN
WHO WEAR
GLASSES

by Shirley Day
illustrated by Don Morris

MAGINATION PRESS • WASHINGTON, DC
American Psychological Association

Luna thought she was named after a fish.

All she could think was "Luna the Tuna." Oh why wasn't she named Alex or Rachel or Sharon?

Luna liked Plato her tiger cat. And she liked her yellow shirt with squiggly lines and circles. And she really liked the arched window in her bedroom where she watched the moon before she went to sleep.

But Luna did NOT like her name. And she didn't like one other thing. Something she could not ignore.

Her eyeglasses.

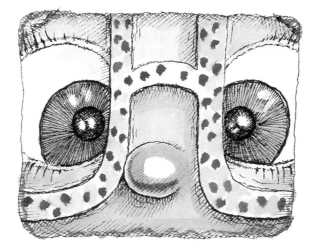

Sitting right on the middle of her nose, making small dents in her face.

Luna got to choose the frames at the eyeglasses store. She picked yellow frames with tiny red polka dots that matched her favorite shirt. But she still didn't like her glasses. When she looked in the mirror, they were all she could see.

She tried to make them less noticeable by covering them up with her bangs.

She tried wearing her coat with her collar up.

She even tried walking around with her head tilted to
the ground. Of course that didn't last very long.

"Ouch!"

Luna's mom owned a gift shop that sold the strangest and craziest things. "Simply wild!" customers would say. She had a clock that ran backwards and a string of lights that looked like cream-filled cookies.

Luna's mom did not need to wear glasses.
Her eyesight was perfect.

Luna's dad taught science at the high school. He also had perfect vision and did not need to wear glasses.

Even Luna's sister Kirstin didn't wear glasses.

"I hate wearing glasses," said Luna. "Even with my favorite clothes, my glasses stick out. **It's not fair.**"

One night as Luna soundly slept, she dreamed that she
was on the moon, surrounded by huge sunflowers next
to a pond filled with hundreds of little, jumping fish.
She could see each fish clearly as it leaped out into the air.

But the best part of her dream was that
she wasn't wearing glasses.

"I can see! No more glasses!"

When she woke up, Luna did not
reach for her glasses. Instead she
left her room cheerfully chanting,
"I can see! No more glasses!"

"Look, Plato, no glasses," she said
as she bent down to pet her
mom's fuzzy slippers. "Oops."

Luna headed to the kitchen. Something smelled yummy. She grabbed a spoon and dipped it into what she thought was a bowl of soup.

"Luna, your spoon is in the fishbowl!" said her mom.

Luna found the ice cream in the freezer and scooped some Peanut Butter Delight into the bowl. She decided to top it off with some fudge syrup. She grabbed the plastic bottle and began to squeeze. Thick gobs of ketchup squirted out.

"Gross!" she yelled.

Luna still wanted a snack. "Oooh, cookies," she said as she grabbed an open bag on the counter.

She was just about to put cat treats in her mouth, when "MMMEOOOWWW!" Plato pressed his nose against Luna's.

"Eeeew! Double gross!" she cried.

All day long, Luna tried hard to see. No matter how she squinted and stared, everything was still a **big blur.** She saw a blur on the sidewalk when she tripped over a pair of roller skates. The blurs in the living room turned into furniture when she bumped into them. Worst of all, the harder she tried to see, the more her head ached.
It finally dawned on her. Her happy dream wasn't true. She couldn't see without her glasses.

Luna headed to her room to put on her glasses and to get ready for bed. Along the way, she poked fun at herself. She sang,

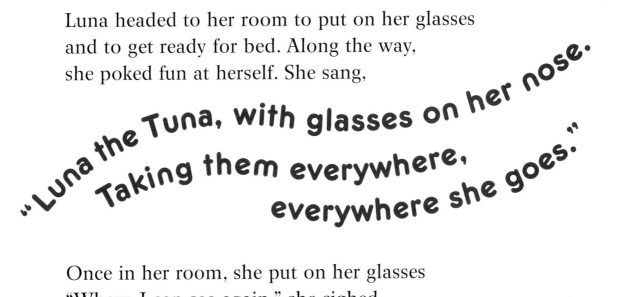

"Luna the Tuna, with glasses on her nose. Taking them everywhere, everywhere she goes."

Once in her room, she put on her glasses "Whew. I can see again," she sighed.

She looked around and yes, she could see again, but she didn't feel so happy.

Luna's dad heard her go upstairs and came up to say good night. "Luna, are you okay?" he asked.

"I don't know, Dad. I had this dream" said Luna, "about the moon and huge sunflowers and little fish. I was so happy because I could see clearly without my glasses. Nothing was blurry. I know that I need my glasses. It's just, why am I the only one in our family who needs to wear them?"

"Oh Luna," said her dad. "Your eyes are different from my eyes and your mom's and Kirstin's. You were born nearsighted. You can see okay up close but not far away. The lenses on your glasses help you focus because the lenses in your eyes can't."

"Besides glasses," said her dad,
"there are other things that
make you different."

"Like what?" Luna asked with a sniffle.

"Well, like your charming personality."

"Oh, Dad."

"And your wit. You're very clever and so curious about everything. Sometimes I wonder if I can answer your questions!

"And," her dad continued "You're the only one in the family named after a certain object in the sky. One that's truly magical."

"Really?" Luna didn't understand.

"Yes, Luna is the name of the moon goddess."

"You named me after the moon?" Luna asked in delight.

"You better believe it, sweetheart," said her dad. "You see, one day before you were born, Mom and I were decorating your room. It was almost midnight when we got through. So we sat down to rest, and there, up in the sky, was a beautiful full moon shining through the window. We decided right then to name you Luna."

Luna was elated. "You mean you didn't name me after a fish?"

"Of course not," said her dad. "And now, back to this business about your glasses…"

"It's okay, Dad. I don't mind wearing my glasses anymore." Luna gave her dad a hug and crawled under the blanket.

"Good night, Dad."

"Sweet dreams, Luna."

Luna removed her glasses from her face and wiped the lenses on the sleeve of her flannel pajamas.

Plato hopped on her bed and curled by her side. From her bed, Luna stared at the big round moon in the sky, surrounded by tiny, flickering stars.

**Glasses or not,
her world
never looked better.**

Note to Parents
by David F. Plotsky, M.D.

Long ago, when I got my first glasses in fifth grade, kids could choose only between black frames and frames with black on top and clear plastic below, hardly a nod to high style in either case. Today, with thousands of styles and colors available, glasses have become a desirable fashion accessory, so much so that many children happily anticipate the day when they need glasses. (Ironically, many ophthalmologists find themselves spending a good deal of time explaining to children who want but do not need glasses that they will be OK without them.)

In spite of this, you may feel anxious for your child when your doctor hands you your child's first glasses prescription. Do not despair! With your understanding and patience, your child will wear his glasses for enough hours every day to achieve the necessary results: seeing the chalkboard in class well, playing more safely, and enjoying seeing the world clearly.

Glasses may be prescribed for children as young as six months of age. Until the age of about five years, most children will generally wear their glasses if they can see more clearly with glasses. Five- to ten-year-olds frequently try to get out of wearing their glasses for many reasons, such as not wanting to look different from peers. To your child, seeing clearly with glasses is probably less important than his appearance or fitting in with his peers. Talking to your child's eye doctor about when the glasses should be worn will help you know how much you need to press the issue with your child.

Specific Ophthalmic Conditions Your Child May Have

In the story, Luna gets her first pair of glasses for nearsightedness (*myopia*). She and her parents confront issues that are commonly encountered by children of her age and with her eye condition. Other concerns and challenges may be expected in children of other ages and with other ophthalmic conditions that require glasses, including:

- Farsightedness (*hyperopia*)
- Imperfection in the curvature of the eye (*astigmatism*)
- Lazy eye (*amblyopia*)
- A significant difference in refraction between the two eyes (*anisometropia*)
- Crossed eyes (*strabismus*).

Nearsightedness (myopia)

Being nearsighted, Luna appreciates the immediate improvement in vision clarity that her glasses provide. This is typical with myopia; your child should experience the same when wearing her glasses.

Farsightedness (hyperopia) and Astigmatism

Highly farsighted or astigmatic children often find themselves in the eye doctor's office after failing vision screening tests at school or at the pediatrician's office. If your child has either of these conditions, her moderately decreased vision will probably not improve when she first wears her glasses. You should talk to your child about this and let her know that if she wears the glasses, her vision will improve over time. You might even work out a compromise to get her used to wearing her glasses. For instance, she doesn't have to wear her glasses when she's playing outside, but she needs to wear them when she's inside.

Lazy Eye (amblyopia)

Lazy eye is a leading cause of vision impairment in children and usually begins in infancy or childhood. If your child has a lazy eye, the condition should improve once he's been wearing his glasses for a while. Your child's eye doctor may also use other treatments to correct his lazy eye, such as drops and patching.

Your child will probably object to using the patch, as many children do, but the importance of its use cannot be overestimated. Your child might feel different for having to wear a patch when his peers do not and he may even be teased by peers for the patch. When your child gets frustrated with the patch or becomes upset with how it makes him look, acknowledge his feelings and remind him that the patching is temporary and will correct his condition.

Remember that though your child may not notice any immediate visual benefit, use of the glasses is very important for strengthening and correcting his eyes. It's also important to keep in mind that once children reach the age of eight or nine, their visual development is complete and concerns about lazy eye should be less worrisome. Once your child's vision is the best it can be with his glasses, his improved vision will stabilize so there is a very low risk of him losing any of his visual acuity.

Anisometropia

In *anisometropia*, your child experiences a marked difference between her two eyes such that the visual development in one eye may lag significantly behind the other. For example, if one eye is myopic and the other hyperopic, vision may be poor in one eye. When glasses are started in this situation, vision may be no better with them on. Full-time wear of glasses (often in conjunction with patching) is needed to improve the vision in the "bad" eye. From your child's perspective, there is no clear advantage to wearing glasses. She might think, "If I can't see better with them, why bother?" When your child gets frustrated with the lack of noticeable improvement in her vision, try gently reminding her that in the long run, the glasses and patching will help her see very well.

Crossed eyes (strabismus)

Children with crossed eyes, or ocular misalignment, may complain of ocular discomfort, headache, blurred vision, or, less commonly, double vision. Glasses will affect your child's eye position by changing his reaction to focus. Because your child may experience some discomfort from his crossed eyes, he might need eye drops or ointment along with his glasses. The expectation is that with glasses on, the your child's eyes will be straight, but when the glasses come off, the misalignment will still be present.

Most likely, your child's vision will be good without glasses, so you should anticipate some difficulty in getting him to wear them. Fortunately, when the glasses are effective in correcting crossed eyes, they are usually well-accepted by children.

Persistence and Compromise

How much your child wears his glasses will vary according to his age and temperament. Explaining the need to improve vision in one eye may work if he is six or seven years old, but it's a very different story with your two-year-old. Persistence is important: reinforcing the notion that glasses are necessary as you return them to his face will ultimately result in an acceptable level of success. In general, full-time wear of glasses is needed for most conditions. But remember, some wear is better than no wear—compromise can be an acceptable and successful strategy.

Although getting your children to wear their glasses after age nine may be difficult, the likelihood that long term visual problems will result from inadequate wear is very low. How the glasses are worn may be tailored to visual needs. To determine your child's specific needs, you should consider the following:

- Is she doing well in school?
- Can he see the board clearly?
- Does he have problems clearly reading his books?
- Is she active in sports like softball or tennis where clear vision is very important?

If his vision without glasses is poor, you might consider getting him sports glasses, as well. They may be very helpful even when the ball is big (as in soccer or basketball) or when there is no ball involved (like in track and field). Sports glasses for vision and protection are increasingly important after age six because the risk that contact will cause regular (everyday) eyewear to break and facial or eye injury increases as the children get bigger and faster.

If she's a swimmer, prescription swimming goggles are available. They may be quite useful to children who spend many hours a day in the pool and do not see well without their glasses.

Kids' Participation

Buying glasses for your children may be a significant positive event in and of itself. The selection that children make often leads to better compliance. You should seek some input from your child regarding the type and style of glasses she'd like. Work with her to look for frames that are not too delicate or flashy, and consider cable temples (earpieces that hook around ears) if your child is particularly active. These frames will stay in place even while hanging upside down, which should make any kid who likes playing on monkey bars happy!

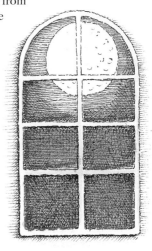

Dealing with Peers

You might want to talk to you child about how his glasses may make them appear different from some of his classmates. At any age, it is helpful for children to understand that wearing glasses may make them appear different from some of their classmates. Although there should not be negative connotations associated with this difference, for some children this is not always the case.

With most children, "a wait and see approach" is probably the best strategy to take for beginning this discussion. If you detect a concern about how the glasses will affect him and his self-esteem, you should approach the issue. On the other hand, if your child seems upbeat or neutral about glasses, you may not need to have the discussion. Surprisingly, these days when a child shows up in elementary school wearing her new glasses there is often a dramatic increase in visual complaints and expressed need for glasses among the classmates.

David F. Plotsky, M.D., is an ophthalmologist specializing in pediatric ophthalmology and adult strabismus in Bethesda, Maryland. He devotes substantial non-clinical time to teaching and training future ophthalmologists. He currently teaches at the Washington Hospital Center where he was past Section Chief of Pediatric Ophthalmology and is on the teaching staff of Children's Hospital in Washington, D.C., and Georgetown University.

About the Author

SHIRLEY DAY lives in San Diego, California, where she is working on more children's books.

About the Illustrator

DON MORRIS works for the *St. Petersburg (Florida) Times* as an illustrator. He has illustrated multiple children's books.